Mr. Putter & Tabby
Dance the Dance

CYNTHIA RYLANT

Mr. Putter & Tabby
Dance the Dance

Illustrated by

ARTHUR HOWARD

Harcourt Children's Books

Houghton Mifflin Harcourt
Boston   New York   2012

Harcourt Children's Books is an imprint of
Houghton Mifflin Harcourt Publishing Company.
www.hmhbooks.com

The illustrations in this book were done in pencil, watercolor,
and gouache on 250-gram cotton rag paper.
The text type was set in Berkeley Old Style Book.
The display type was set in Minya Nouvelle, Agenda, and Artcraft.

Library of Congress Cataloging-in-Publication Data

Rylant, Cynthia.
Mr. Putter & Tabby dance the dance / Cynthia Rylant;
illustrated by Arthur Howard.
p. cm.
ISBN 978-0-15-206415-0
[1. Ballroom dancing—Fiction. 2. Neighbors—Fiction. 3. Old age—Fiction.
4. Cats—Fiction. 5. Dogs—Fiction.] I. Howard, Arthur, ill. II. Title. III. Title:
Mister Putter & Tabby dance the dance. IV. Title: Mr. Putter and Tabby dance
the dance.
PZ7.R982Msck 2012
[E]—dc23
2011041934

Manufactured in China
LEO 1 3 5 7 9 10 8 6 4 2
4500361787

1

A New Thing

Mr. Putter and his fine cat, Tabby,
liked living next door to
Mrs. Teaberry and her good dog, Zeke.
They all had a lot of things in common.

They all liked the Sunday funnies.

They all liked cheese toasties.

They all liked rain.

Mrs. Teaberry was good at finding
new things for them to like.
Sometimes the new things worked.

Sometimes they didn't.

Lately Mrs. Teaberry had been
watching a contest on television.
It was a dancing contest.
The dancing was called ballroom
dancing, and it looked like fun.

Mrs. Teaberry called Mr. Putter.
"I think we should go
ballroom dancing," she said.

Mr. Putter looked at Tabby,
who was napping in the geranium.
Tabby was old, like he was.
She loved to nap.
So did he.

"I'm not sure I have it in me,"
Mr. Putter told Mrs. Teaberry.
"I haven't danced since 1947."

"Dancing is good for people,"
said Mrs. Teaberry.

"It gets them all loosey-goosey."

"Loosey-goosey?" asked Mr. Putter.

"Just try it," said Mrs. Teaberry.

"What have you got to lose?"

Mr. Putter could think of a lot
of things he had to lose.
Like his dignity. And his nap time.
But Mr. Putter never wanted
to say no to Mrs. Teaberry.
She was his good friend.

"All right," said Mr. Putter.
"But I have two left feet.
I won't be very good at it."
"You are a wonder at *everything*,"
said Mrs. Teaberry.

Mr. Putter smiled.

He liked being a wonder.

It was nice to have a friend

who thought so.

2

Sparkles

Mr. Putter and Tabby
and Mrs. Teaberry and Zeke
went to the Crystal Ballroom.
It was very nice.
It had sparkly lights and
a sparkly floor.
Everyone there looked
very sparkly, too.

Tabby loved it.

She batted at the sparkles.

"Do you know how to foxtrot?"
Mrs. Teaberry asked Mr. Putter.

"Afraid not," said Mr. Putter.

"Do you know how to rumba?"
asked Mrs. Teaberry.

"Afraid not," said Mr. Putter.

"Do you know how to *one-two-cha-cha-cha*?"
asked Mrs. Teaberry.

"That I can do," Mr. Putter said.

They went out on the dance floor.

They told Tabby and Zeke to stay.

One of them was good at staying.

One of them was not.

3

Dancing!

Zeke ran out to the dance floor.
He grabbed a man's tuxedo tails
and danced with him awhile.

Then he grabbed a lady's poodle skirt
and danced with her awhile.

Then he jumped into a tango
and really let go!

He even got the rose right.

Everyone watched Zeke tango.

No one watched Mr. Putter
cha-cha-cha, which was good
because Mr. Putter had two left feet.
But he was having fun.
Everyone was having fun!

The orchestra played,
the dancers danced,
Zeke tangoed,

and a very happy cat
batted the sparkles!

When the night was over,
Tabby and Zeke got lots
of leftover pretzels and fizzy water.
(Even the ballroom water was sparkly!)

And Zeke got to keep his rose.

Everyone went home happy.

Everyone went home humming.

Everyone went home dancing a little dance.

They all felt like wonders.

Mr. Putter most of all.